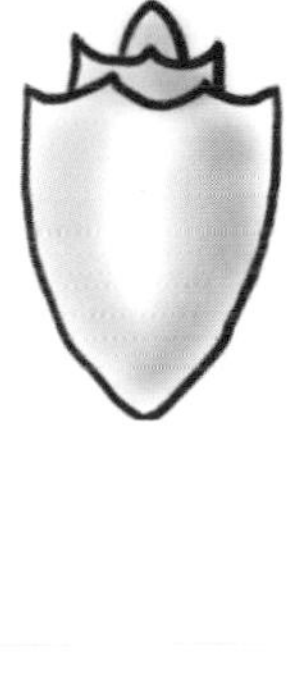

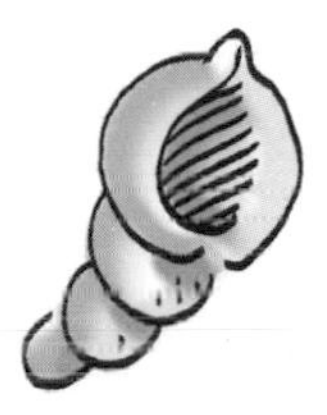

Summer the Holiday Fairy was originally published as a Rainbow Magic special. This version has been specially adapted for developing readers in conjunction with a Reading Consultant.

Special thanks to
Rachel Elliot, Fiona Munro
and Linda Chapman

Reading Consultant: Prue Goodwin, lecturer in literacy and children's books.

ORCHARD BOOKS

This story first published in Great Britain in 2005 by Orchard Books
First published as an Early Reader in 2013
This edition published in 2019 by The Watts Publishing Group

1 3 5 7 9 10 8 6 4 2

© 2019 Rainbow Magic Limited.
© 2019 HIT Entertainment Limited.
Illustrations © Orchard Books 2013

The moral rights of the author and illustrator have been asserted.
All characters and events in this publication, other than those clearly in the public domain, are fictitious and any resemblance to real persons, living or dead, is purely coincidental.

All rights reserved.
No part of this publication may be reproduced, stored in a retrieval system, or transmitted, in any form or by any means, without the prior permission in writing of the publisher, nor be otherwise circulated in any form of binding or cover other than that in which it is published and without a similar condition including this condition being imposed on the subsequent purchaser.

A CIP catalogue record for this book is available from the British Library.

ISBN 978 1 40835 980 8

Printed in China

The paper and board used in this book are made from wood from responsible sources

Orchard Books
An imprint of Hachette Children's Group
Part of The Watts Publishing Group Limited
Carmelite House, 50 Victoria Embankment, London EC4Y 0DZ

An Hachette UK Company
www.hachette.co.uk
www.hachettechildrens.co.uk

Summer
the Holiday Fairy

Daisy Meadows

www.rainbowmagicbooks.co.uk

The Fairyland Palace
Maze
Orchard
Black Pot
Meadow
Tower
Beach
Rockpools
Rainspell Island

Jack Frost's
Ice Castle
Stream
Field
Town
Harbour
Dolphin Cottage

Story One

The Curly Twirly Shell

It was the start of the summer holidays. Rachel, her best friend Kirsty and their parents were all heading off to Rainspell Island.

"Have you finished packing yet?" Mrs Walker called.

"Almost!" Rachel replied.

Rachel and Kirsty had first met on holiday on Rainspell Island and had an amazing secret. They were friends with the fairies and had shared so many adventures. Maybe they would have one on this holiday!

"Oh no!" Rachel groaned, pulling her favourite T-shirt from under her bed. It was dirty! She sighed and went to get her washbag. When Rachel came back, she gasped. The T-shirt was sparkly clean! Bending closer, she saw a tiny, glowing footprint on the sleeve. "Fairy dust!" she whispered.

A car horn beeped outside. Kirsty and her parents had arrived! Rachel ran downstairs.

"Sorry we're late!" Kirsty's mum said. "The car had a flat tyre when we got up this morning."

"But by the time I'd fetched my tools, it wasn't flat any more," Mr Tate said. "Almost like magic!"

Rachel and Kirsty looked at each other.

"Kirsty, come and see my new duvet cover," Rachel suggested.

She was bursting to tell Kirsty what had happened.

The girls raced upstairs as Rachel's words tumbled out. "I bet your car tyre was fixed by magic," she whispered. "A fairy's been here too!"

A few hours later, the ferry was chugging its way across the flat green sea.

"I can't wait to get to Rainspell Island," Rachel said.

"There it is!" Kirsty pointed at a rocky island in the distance. Suddenly, she shivered. "Brrr! The sun's gone in!"

"And the sea's getting rougher," Rachel said. "I bet Jack Frost's up to something again."

Just then, a big wave tossed the boat upwards. Kirsty stumbled, and bumped into a pile of rope. As she tried to find her feet again, she heard a tiny tinkling sound.

The sound was coming from under the pile of rope. It was a fairy! She was wearing a yellow top with a matching yellow-and-orange sarong.

"You must be Rachel and Kirsty," said the fairy. "I'm Summer the Holiday Fairy. Jack Frost has made the sea turn rough! He's trying to wreck all holidays because he wants Rainspell Island all for himself." She smiled. "Did you notice I'd been at your houses today?"

Rachel and Kirsty beamed at each other. They knew it had been magic!

Suddenly, Summer's wand made a tinkling sound. "Oh my!" she cried. "There's an emergency on Rainspell!" She flew off in a burst of golden fairy dust.

When the ferry arrived at Rainspell Island, the sky was

blue again and the girls were feeling excited. But everyone else was looking unhappy. When

they reached the beach they found out why. There was no sand! Just pebbles and rocks.

"There was a terrible storm," a man passing by told them. "When it was over the sand was gone."

There was no ice cream either! The ice cream seller told the Tates and Walkers that it just kept melting and tasted horrible.

"Oh, goodness!" said Mrs Walker. "This isn't going to be much of a holiday."

After reaching their holiday cottage and unpacking, Rachel and Kirsty walked along the empty beach. As Kirsty picked up a pebble to toss into the sea, a shower of golden dust flew into the air. It was Summer!

"Hi there!" called the fairy. "Jack Frost's magic has taken all the shells!"

"But why?" Rachel asked.

"I'll show you," said Summer. She raised her golden wand and swirled the girls up in a cloud of shimmering fairy dust. Rachel and Kirsty could feel themselves shrinking to fairy-size.

"We're fairies again!" they cried. They flew up into the bright blue sky.

The girls swooped to the other side of the island. They followed Summer as she dived down and hovered on the spot. Beneath them was an enormous sandcastle, decorated with thousands of shells. This was where all the sand and shells had gone! The sandcastle belonged to Jack Frost.

"Jack Frost has stolen the three magic Rainspell shells," said Summer.

The little fairy explained that the first shell makes the food on Rainspell taste delicious. The second shell controls the wind and waves. The third shell looks after beaches.

"If I could return the shells to their special cave, Rainspell would go back to normal again," Summer told the girls.

The fairies noticed that the goblins guarding the sandcastle were eating ice creams. Apart from one, who was standing further away, and grumbling.

Just then, Kirsty saw a large twirly shell sparkle. It was in the sandcastle wall, next to the grumbling goblin.

"That's a Rainspell shell!" Summer cried.

"We need to distract that goblin to reach it," said Rachel.

Fluttering up to the surprised goblin, Rachel told him she knew where there was lots of ice cream. As he ran off after Rachel, Summer and Kirsty fluttered down. They pulled the magic shell from the wall.

Summer thanked the girls for helping her find the first Rainspell shell. She told them that she must put the shell back in an underwater cave, where the shells are usually kept.

Summer flicked her wand. In a cloud of fairy dust the girls shot up to human-size. Back on Rainspell beach, they walked towards the ice cream seller.

"My ice cream machine's working again! Would you like one?" the seller called.

"Yes, please!" replied the girls.

"We must help Summer rescue the other Rainspell shells," Kirsty said to Rachel.

"Don't worry," Rachel replied. "We'll soon make Rainspell Island perfect again!"

Story Two

The Sea Breeze Shell

The Sea Breeze Shell

"It's a wonderful day for the Rainspell boat race!" Kirsty said as she pulled on her trainers. Mr Walker and Mr Tate were entering the race. Everyone was very excited.

The two families walked towards the harbour together.

"It's very hot," said Mr Walker. "I hope a breeze picks up, or the boats won't be able to sail."

The families joined the crowds of people at the harbour.

"Let's ask the harbour master what's happening," said Mr Tate.

"I think the race might have to be cancelled," the man said.

Rachel and Kirsty asked if

they could go to the beach. They ran across the pebbles.

"This is Jack Frost's fault," said Kirsty. "He's got the magic shell that controls the wind!"

Suddenly, Summer appeared in front of the girls in a fountain of golden sparks.

"How are you?" asked Summer. Rachel told her all about the problem with the wind at the boat race.

"Oh dear," began Summer. "Jack Frost blew the magic shell this morning, so all the wind would go to his side of the island for his own race."

"What can we do?" asked Kirsty.

"He's put the magic shell on one of his sandcastle turrets, and we need to rescue it!" said Summer. She waved her wand and a cloud of golden dust floated over the girls. They turned into fairies again.

The three fairies flew over the island until they arrived at Jack Frost's sandcastle. Loud yells were coming from the beach. The goblins were sailing in a strange collection of boats made from blow-up toys and beach towels! They were crashing into each other and shouting.

Kirsty looked back at the sandcastle. The top of each tower was decorated with pretty shells.

"One of those is the magic sea breeze shell," said Summer. "But I'm not sure which one. How are we going to know?"

Just then, the sun came out and one shell began to glow.

"That has to be the magic one!" whispered Kirsty.

"It is!" said Summer. "It always glitters in the sun. Let's sneak into the sandcastle while all the goblins are sailing. Then we can take the shell and put it back where it belongs."

"Okay," said Rachel. "Let's find a shell that looks like the magic one, and swap them over!" She flew over to the sand and grabbed a shell from under the nose of some goblins.

Then, the three fairies flew into the sandcastle while the guards were watching the race.

They fluttered up the tower and peeped round the door.

"We made it!" Summer said.

"Come on, quick! Let's swap the shells and get out," replied Kirsty.

"But which is the magic shell?" Rachel asked. The sun had gone behind a cloud, and without it the shells all looked exactly the same! The three fairies thought very hard. What could they do?

Suddenly, Summer waved her wand. It sent a golden glow like a torch beam through the grey air, lighting up one of the shells.

Rachel quickly pulled it out of the wall and Kirsty stuck the new shell in its place. With racing hearts, they flew down the stairs. Straight into the path of a big green goblin with a warty nose!

Summer gasped as the goblin ran past them. She grabbed Rachel and Kirsty's arms and flew up to the ceiling with them.

"Come on, let's get out of here before Jack Frost realises he's been tricked!" Summer said. So they zoomed out of the door and up into the air.

Suddenly, the girls heard a yell so loud that it made the sandcastle walls shake.

"WHAT'S THIS?"

"Quick!" Summer looked scared. "I think Jack Frost has just found out that the magic shell has gone!"

"Pesky fairies!" Jack Frost shouted out of his window.

"Come back here with my magic shell!"

With a final look back at the sandcastle, the girls and Summer flew away.

"Phew!" Rachel said as they reached Rainspell harbour. "That was scary!"

"But at least you rescued the magic shell!" Summer grinned. "Do you want to come to the underwater cave and help me put it back where it belongs?"

Rachel and Kirsty looked at the boats bobbing on the calm sea.

"We should get back," Rachel said. "We told our mums that we'd meet them to watch the boat race."

Kirsty glanced at the big clock on the harbour wall. Almost half an hour had passed since they had left their parents with the harbour master.

"It doesn't look like there's going to be a race, though." Rachel sighed. "There's not enough wind for sailing."

"Oh, you need the wind right now?" Summer asked.

Rachel and Kirsty nodded.

Summer raised the magic shell to her lips. At once, a breeze swirled across the beach.

With each of Summer's breaths, the wind grew stronger, until the sails of the boats were flapping in the breeze.

Lowering the shell, Summer smiled at Rachel and Kirsty.

"Thanks, Summer!" the girls said together.

"No problem!" said the fairy. She waved her wand and a cloud of fairy dust floated around the girls. They shot back up to their normal size.

"The race must be about to start!" Kirsty said.

Waving goodbye to Summer the two girls ran across the pebble beach.

"Come on, Dad!" they both shouted. Their dads' boat raced towards the finishing line, just in front of the others!

"They've won!" called Mrs

Walker and Mrs Tate.

"Just one more shell to rescue," Kirsty whispered to Rachel.

Rachel grinned. "We'll get it back. I know we will!"

Story Three

The Magic Scallop Shell

The sun was shining as Rachel and Kirsty ran down to Rainspell beach. It was a perfect day for donkey riding!

"It's very quiet," said Kirsty.

"It just isn't the same without the sand," agreed Rachel.

"We have to get the last Rainspell shell back," said Kirsty.

Ever since Jack Frost had stolen the sand and shells to build his sandcastle, people had stayed away from the beach.

The girls spotted Mr Williams and his four fluffy donkeys. He was checking one of the

donkey's hooves.

"Hello," Kirsty called. "Can we have a ride, please?"

Mr Williams shook his head. "I'm afraid not. The beach is too rocky. Pippin has hurt her hoof. There won't be any more donkey rides while the beach is like this." He sighed. "I'd better take them back to their field."

"Jack Frost is determined to spoil everyone's holiday, isn't he?" Rachel said sadly.

Suddenly, Kirsty gasped. "Look!"

A cloud of golden dust whooshed up from behind a rock and Summer the Holiday Fairy flew towards the girls.

"I've found out where Jack Frost is keeping the third magic Rainspell shell!" Summer cried.

"He's using it to decorate his throne in the Great Hall. If we don't put it back in its underwater cave soon, the beaches on Rainspell will stay sandless for ever!"

"We can't let that happen," said Rachel.

Kirsty nodded. "We're not going to give up!"

Summer waved her wand, showering Rachel and Kirsty with fairy dust. At once they shrank to fairy-size. Together, they flew across the island.

"Jack Frost was so angry about losing the other two shells he's put extra guards on duty," Summer warned.

Sure enough, when they reached the sandcastle, there were goblins everywhere.

Kirsty noticed that the windows looked freezing cold.

"The windows are made of ice," Summer told them. "Jack Frost has put a spell on them so they won't melt in the sun. But my special summer magic can make a hole just big enough for us to get through."

Kirsty and Rachel watched as Summer's wand glowed. It melted a tiny hole in one of the icy windows.

Summer looked pale as she concentrated on making the

hole bigger. "Jack Frost's spell is strong," she said quietly. "There's not much magic left in my wand."

When the hole was big enough, Rachel and Kirsty followed Summer inside. They flew to the Great Hall. Rachel pushed the door open and they saw a magnificent throne with a glowing shell stuck to the very top.

"It's the magic scallop shell!" Summer whispered. She picked it up.

"Stop right there!" A cold voice snapped. It was Jack Frost!

"Quick! Melt the window, Summer!" Kirsty cried.

Summer raced to the window and touched the pane with her wand. There wasn't much magic left, so the girls were relieved when the ice melted.

"Let's go!" Kirsty said, flying into the air with Rachel.

But poor, tired Summer just lay on the window ledge.

Trying not to panic, Kirsty grabbed the shell. Rachel put her arms around the exhausted little fairy to help her.

"Quick, Rachel, through the window!" said Kirsty.

Just then, Jack Frost raised his hands. Icy bolts flew from his fingertips. The window froze over with a fresh sheet of glittering ice!

Kirsty thought hard. "Follow me," she called to Rachel. "We'll go back the way we came in!"

Carrying Summer and the shell, the two girls flew across the room and out of the door.

"Stop those fairies NOW!"

Jack Frost yelled to the goblins.

With a final effort, Kirsty and Rachel climbed through the hole in the window they had come through earlier. Luckily, it hadn't frozen over again! They stood outside on the window ledge.

"We can't stay here," Rachel said. "The goblins will see us!"

"But we can't fly carrying both the shell and Summer," worried Kirsty.

"Are you all right?" came a voice. They looked up and saw a seagull flying towards them.

"Summer's used up all her magic," Rachel explained to the friendly looking bird.

"We need to take the magic shell back to the underwater cave," added Kirsty.

"Climb on my back. I'll fly you to the sea," the kind seagull said.

Rachel and Kirsty climbed on. They lifted Summer and the magic shell onto the seagull's back.

"You pesky fairies!" came Jack Frost's cold voice from a window behind them. "Bring back that shell!"

"Never!" Rachel shouted.

By the time the seagull landed on the sea, Summer had started to wake up. She felt much better. The little fairy looked in her beach bag and pulled out a sparkling pink bottle.

"It's fairy bubble mixture," she explained, blowing three big bubbles and handing one each to Rachel and Kirsty. "Put these onto your heads."

The bubbles sank down until their heads were covered. Now they could all breathe underwater!

The three of them said thank you and goodbye to the seagull. Then Summer suddenly cried, "JUMP!"

The girls jumped. Rachel, Kirsty and Summer went down, down, down into the deep water.

"Wow!" said Kirsty. An underwater cave had appeared ahead, with three stone shelves on the wall. Two shelves held the shells they had already found at Jack Frost's sandcastle. Summer carefully put the third magic shell onto the last empty shelf.

At once, a fountain of sparkles fizzed through the water. They heard a low rumbling noise.

"I think that was Jack Frost's sandcastle falling down," gasped Summer. "And look, my wand has filled up with magic!"

Rachel, Kirsty and Summer swam back up to the surface and saw that soft sand now lay where the sandcastle had stood.

"Look!" Rachel pointed as they flew back to their side of the island. They could see golden sand all around.

"Thanks for helping me," Summer said. She turned the girls back to human-size.

Rachel and Kirsty went back to their holiday home. There they found shiny swimsuits on their beds.

"They must be from Summer!" said Kirsty.

Laughing, the two girls raced across the soft sand and splashed into the warm sea. It was going to be a great holiday, after all!

If you enjoyed this story, you may want to read

Shannon the Ocean Fairy Early Reader

Here's how the story begins...

Rachel Walker and her best friend Kirsty Tate raced across Leamouth beach, laughing. They were on holiday together, staying with Kirsty's gran.

Down where the waves lapped onto the sand, the girls noticed a beautiful seashell. They gasped as a burst of pale blue sparkles fizzed out of it.

"Fairy magic!" Kirsty whispered. Their friendship with the fairies was a special secret.

"Hello, girls," said a voice from the shell.

It was the fairy queen!

"We'd like to invite you to a special beach party," said Queen Titania. "I hope you can come."

Suddenly, a rainbow shot out from the shell. When the two friends stepped onto it, they disappeared in a whirl of fairy magic.

The girls had been turned into fairies! They were standing on a different beach now. It was crowded with fairies enjoying a party. King Oberon and Queen Titania welcomed them.

"The tide's coming in. Will the party end soon?" Rachel asked a nearby fairy. It was Shannon the Ocean Fairy! She was wearing a pink skirt and had a glittering starfish clip in her hair.

"No. The sea never comes beyond Party Rock." Shannon

smiled, pointing to a large boulder.

Just then, the party music stopped.

"The sea's coming in too far!" called Shannon. "Something's wrong!"

Read
Shannon the Ocean Fairy
Early Reader
to find out
what happens next!

EARLY READER

RAINBOW magic™

Support your child's reading journey with the Rainbow Magic Fairies

Meet the first Rainbow Magic fairies

Can you find one with your name?
There's a fairy book for everyone at
www.rainbowmagicbooks.co.uk

Let the magic begin!

Become a

Rainbow Magic

fairy friend and be the first to see sneak peeks of new books.

There are lots of special offers and exclusive competitions to win sparkly Rainbow Magic prizes.

Sign up today at
www.rainbowmagicbooks.co.uk